FICTION

Voices in the Dark

Jan Carew

First published in 2001 by:
Nelson Thornes Ltd
Delta Place
27 Bath Road
CHELTENHAM
GL53 7TH
United Kingdom

01   02   03   04   05   /   10   9   8   7   6   5   4   3   2   1

A catalogue record for this book is available from the British Library.

ISBN 0-7487-6060-1

Cover artwork by Martin Berry
Typeset by Tech-Set Ltd, Gateshead
Printed and bound in Great Britain by Martins The Printers Ltd, Berwick upon Tweed

1

Kate Smith looked round the London office and sighed. Her boss had left it in a mess as usual. Dan Harper was a great detective but he was no good at paperwork. Now he had gone off to Australia for a long holiday and left her to tidy up. The office was going to be closed till Dan came back. Kate thought she'd better make a start.

Suddenly, there was a tap on the door. Kate could see someone on the other side of the frosted glass. Kate went to the door and opened it. A young woman with fair hair stood there. She looked very nervous. Kate wondered why.

'I'm sorry,' she said to the visitor. 'The office is closed. Mr Harper is away. I'm his secretary. I can't help you.'

The woman's face fell. She looked really disappointed. Kate was afraid she was going to cry.

'Why don't you come in and sit down?' Kate said gently. 'I'm just making a cup of tea. Would you like one?'

The girl nodded and tried to smile. She was very pretty but her blue eyes were full of fear. Kate wondered what she was worried about. Over a cup of tea, she got the girl to talk.

'My name is Julie Rogers,' the girl began. 'I'm a singer with a rock band. It's called Easy Money. Maybe you haven't heard of us yet. We've done a lot of gigs lately.'

'But I *have* heard of you!' said Kate. 'People say you're really good.'

Julie looked pleased. 'We hope to have a hit record soon – with a video.'

Now Kate was really interested. She loved music. 'That's great,' she said. 'I wish you the best of luck, Julie. Have you got a record contract yet?'

Julie's face lit up. 'Yes,' she said. 'Sunset Records are keen to bring out our first record. It's a song called "Voices in the Dark".' Suddenly, Julie looked a bit shy. 'I wrote the words myself. And some of the music as well. Everything has been going so well lately. All my dreams seemed to be coming true. Until . . .'

Julie stopped talking and the fear came back to her face. Her eyes looked haunted.

'What's wrong, Julie?' Kate asked. 'Why are you so frightened?'

6

Julie gulped some of her tea. 'I don't know what to do,' she said. 'I was hoping Mr Harper could help me. A detective could find out if I'm right or if I'm imagining it all.'

'What?' asked Kate.

Julie looked straight at her. Her blue eyes were very serious.

'Please don't think I'm crazy. I think someone is trying to kill me.'

2

For a moment, Kate didn't know what to say. She hadn't expected this. Some small personal problem perhaps. The sort of thing a detective agency handled all the time. Like a missing person. But not this. Not murder!

Kate tried to think clearly. She couldn't help Julie. After all, she wasn't a detective. But at least she could listen to Julie's story. It might make the girl feel better to have someone to talk to. She looked afraid of her own shadow.

'Tell me all about it, Julie,' Kate said. 'Maybe you're worried about nothing.'

Julie took a deep breath. 'I had an accident a month ago. I was riding my bike. I do it a lot to save train fares. I was on my way to a band practice. We meet in a room over a pub. It was an easy ride there – or so I thought.'

She stopped and Kate saw the scared look on her face again.

'The last bit is downhill. It's quite steep. I felt the bike going too fast so I used my brakes. They didn't work. My bike just rushed down the hill. It was completely out of control. I held on to the handlebars and prayed I wouldn't crash into a lorry or something. There's a busy main road ahead.'

'How terrible!' said Kate. 'What happened?'

'I was lucky,' said Julie. 'I fell off my bike just before I reached the main road. It went straight into a car. I landed in some bushes. I got some bumps and bruises but I was OK.'

'That was lucky,' said Kate. 'I can understand why you were shaken up, but lots of people have accidents. It's over now.'

'Not quite,' said Julie. 'I took the bike to a repair shop. It was in a mess. I wanted to see if it could be mended. But I also wanted to know why the brakes had let me down. Then I got a shock. The man said it looked as if the brake cables had been cut. I couldn't believe it. I thought he must be wrong. But then something else happened to me.'

Kate was very interested now. She told Julie to go on.

'It was at the station. I was waiting for my train. It was the rush hour and the platform was crowded. I heard a train coming but I knew it wasn't the one I wanted. So

I stepped back. Then I felt it. There was a hand on my back, pushing me forward. I tried to get away but there were people all round me. Someone was pushing me to the edge of the platform and I couldn't do a thing about it. Then I heard another train coming. I was terrified. At the last moment, I grabbed a man's arm and held on tight. The train roared past me. It was so close that it ripped my sleeve. I was lucky to be alive. I turned round to see who was behind me. But it was no good. I didn't see who it was.'

Kate thought hard about this. 'That was very scary. But crowds do push and shove in the rush hour. It's a wonder there aren't more accidents. Maybe you imagined the hand on your back.'

Julie looked hopeful. 'Do you think so? But what about my bike?'

Kate was glad to see Julie looking more cheerful.

'Well,' said Kate, 'it was pretty smashed up, wasn't it? It wasn't easy to tell what went wrong. Put it this way, is there any reason why someone would want to kill you? Do you have any enemies?'

'No,' said Julie. 'Not an enemy in the world. We're all great friends in the band. And Easy Money is going places. I know it is. I have every reason to be happy.'

Kate made up her mind. 'Then be happy, Julie. Put these fears out of your mind. I'm sure there's no reason for you to be afraid. Just think of the great future you're going to have as a singer. I'll be the first to buy your new record. What's your song called again?'

'"Voices in the Dark",' said Julie with a smile. The shadow had lifted from her face and Kate was delighted to see it.

As she showed her client out, Kate felt rather proud of her afternoon's work. She still had to tidy the office, but never mind. That could wait till tomorrow. It was more important to set someone's mind at rest.

3

Over the next few weeks, Kate was busy. She went to lots of job interviews. She needed a job as a temp till her boss got back.

One evening, she took a train home. She was feeling very tired. No job seemed to be right for her. She missed her work at the detective agency. There was always something happening there. It made other jobs seem dull.

Kate bought a newspaper to read on the train. She meant to look at the jobs page. But as she turned the pages, something caught her eye. It was a photo of a girl. Kate felt she recognised her. It was Julie Rogers!

Then Kate's heart missed a beat. The headline above the photo read 'Sad death of young singer'. Kate felt sick with shock. She'd only met Julie once but she'd really liked her. After a moment, Kate read the rest of the story. The girl's body had been found in a river. She had drowned at a well known beauty spot near London. It was a quiet place, popular with fishermen. One of them had seen the body and raised the alarm. No one knew how the accident had happened. It was very sad because she was a talented singer. She had no family.

Kate put the newspaper in her bag. She was near the end of her journey. She felt miserable as she walked home from the station. She had told Julie Rogers there was nothing to worry about. She had sent her away happy and with an easy mind.

What if I was wrong, Kate asked herself and feared the answer. She thought again about the accidents that had happened to Julie. She tried to remember all the details.

First there was the bike with faulty brakes. Julie thought they may have been cut. What if she was right?

Then Julie felt that someone had tried to push her under a train. Maybe she hadn't imagined it after all.

It's too much of a coincidence, thought Kate. Julie thought someone was trying to kill her and now she was dead. Another accident?

Kate's face became grim and serious. She felt as if she had let Julie down. She hadn't believed the girl's story. There was only one thing to do now. She would try to find out the truth about Julie's death. Kate would become a detective herself.

4

Kate felt better now. She had made up her mind to do something about Julie's death. She wasn't sure how to go about it though.

Somehow she must get in to the music world Julie belonged to. But how?

Kate read through the list of ads on the jobs page. She did it every night. She wasn't really thinking.

Then a name caught her eye. It was a name she'd heard recently. Sunset Records wanted a typist in their office. Wasn't that the record company Julie spoke about? They were going to release her new disc. Kate felt excited. She had to get the job with Sunset Records. It didn't matter what the pay was like. It would get her close to the people who knew Julie Rogers. Then maybe she could find out something.

Kate dressed with care for the interview the next day. She had to get this job. A young man in a suit interviewed her. His name was David Farley. He seemed nice and very business-like. He asked Kate questions about her typing and her other jobs. Kate said nothing about working in a detective agency.

She felt it was better to keep quiet about that. Mr Farley seemed happy with her answers and gave her the job at once. The pay wasn't very good but it was, as Mr Farley said, interesting work.

'You might even meet the odd pop star,' he joked.

'I certainly hope so,' said Kate – and meant it.

A girl called Trish showed Kate round the office. Trish was leaving and Kate was taking over her job. 'I think you'll find everything in order,' said Trish. 'I've been very happy here and I'm sure you will be. David Farley is a really good boss. He lets you get on with things.'

'He's very young to be the manager, isn't he?' asked Kate.

Trish looked surprised. 'Oh, he's not the manager of Sunset Records. He owns the company. Not that David is rich himself, but he has rich relatives. Do you know who his aunt is?'

Kate shook her head. She had no idea.

'Maria Ridley, the film actress,' said Trish. 'She set him up in business. Some people have all the luck, eh? Mind you, David Farley does know a lot about the music business. It's only a matter of time before Sunset Records will bring out a number one hit.'

Kate thought about 'Voices in the Dark'. What would happen now to Julie's song? Would it still be released?

She was looking forward to Trish going. She needed to be alone in the office. Then she could find all the facts about the rock band Julie had sung in. What was it called again? Oh yes – Easy Money.

At last, Trish left the office. She wished Kate good luck before she went. I'll need it, thought Kate.

She went to the files right away. As Trish said, everything was in order. Kate found the right file easily. The name of the band was on the front. Kate opened it. Then she got a slight shock. There were photos of the four members of the band. And one of them was a picture of Julie. She was smiling and looking really happy. Kate felt sad to think of the girl's death.

Kate looked at the other three people. There was Rob Mason, who played guitar and keyboards. He looked clever and rather sulky. But a lot of pop people did. It was a pose for the camera. There was another young man who played drums. He was called Alan Jarvis. Kate liked the look of him. He had an open, friendly smile. The third person was a pretty black girl called Patsy Summers. She had a warm smile which lit up her eyes.

16

Kate sighed. None of these people looked like a murderer. But what did a murderer look like? They looked just like everyone else. What would a real detective do now, she wondered. What would Dan Harper do?

She knew the answer. He'd go out and meet these people, Kate told herself. And that's just what I'm going to do.

5

It was noisy in the club. Too noisy. Kate hoped the band would play soon. She was here tonight to hear Easy Money.

'Another drink?' asked the barman. Kate shook her head. 'No thanks. I've really come for the music. I hear it's a good band tonight.'

'Yeah,' said the barman. 'I'm quite a fan myself. Haven't you heard them before?'

'No,' said Kate. 'I'm looking forward to it.'

'There's one of them now,' said the barman, looking at the door. Kate turned and saw Alan Jarvis carrying his drum kit. He looked just like his photo – friendly and easy to talk to. Kate decided to have a go.

'Hi!' she said as Alan came over to the bar. 'Can I buy you a drink? I'm one of your fans.'

Alan looked surprised but pleased. He liked the look of this pretty, dark haired girl. 'Thanks,' he said. 'I'll have a Coke.'

Kate and Alan soon got talking. He was as nice as he looked. And very modest about his part in the band. 'Rob is the really musical one,' he said. 'He writes a lot of our songs, along with . . .'

'Yes?' asked Kate.

Alan looked very sad suddenly. 'Along with Julie. She was our lead singer. She died a short time ago.'

'How awful,' said Kate. 'She must have been very young. What happened?'

Alan shook his head. 'I don't want to talk about it,' he said. 'It was a terrible accident. Please don't say anything about it to Rob. He and Julie used to be very close.'

Kate saw why Alan had warned her about Rob. He was on his way over to the bar. Kate was glad to see he looked more friendly than his photo.

'Hi!' said Rob. 'I'm dying of thirst. Can I get you guys another drink?'

Kate was pleased how quickly she had met the band. Now she only had to meet Patsy Summers. She did that at half-time when the band took a break. Patsy was a lively girl, full of fun. She was easy to talk to and soon Kate had a chance to bring up Julie's name.

Patsy's face became serious. She looked really sad. 'Her death was an awful shock,' she said. 'To all of us. Especially Rob. He was crazy about Julie, even after they broke up. Poor guy. He hasn't got over it yet.'

'I wonder why they broke up,' said Kate, hoping she didn't sound too nosey.

Patsy frowned. 'Goodness knows,' she said. 'They got on so well together. They wrote a lot of our songs too. I'm the lead singer now. Of course, I'm glad to get the chance but I didn't want it like this. I feel as if I'm stepping into Julie's shoes. It makes me feel a bit guilty.'

'I know what you mean,' said Kate. 'But you've got a great voice. What's your next song?'

Patsy smiled now. 'It's our new one. We're making a record soon and we think it'll be a hit. It's called "Voices in the Dark".'

Kate listened to the song and thought of all the things she'd learned that night. Quite a lot for a first meeting.

First, Rob had been in love with Julie and she had dumped him. That was enough to make any man hurt and angry. How angry? Enough to kill her?

As for Patsy, she did well out of Julie's death. She was the star singer now. For an unknown young singer like Patsy, that was quite a prize. Enough to kill for?

6

Kate went to every gig to hear the band. She enjoyed it. She was now a real fan of Easy Money.

She looked forward to meeting the band every time. Especially Alan. She liked him more and more. He seemed to like her too. He often sat beside her at break times.

But Rob must be the key to finding out more about Julie. He was her boyfriend till shortly before her death. I wonder why they broke up, Kate asked herself. Was there another man in Julie's life? The girl said she felt that all her dreams were coming true. That could have meant she was in love with someone. But who?

That night, Kate had a chance to speak to Rob alone. He stayed behind after the others had left. He looked like he was feeling low and was staring at his drink. Kate sat down beside him.

'Another drink, Rob?' she asked.

'Why not?' he said. 'Not that it helps. It doesn't bring her back. Nothing can do that.'

Kate decided to be bold. 'You mean Julie?' she said. Rob looked surprised.

'I didn't know you knew her.'

Kate crossed her fingers under the table and told a lie.

'I used to know her when we were kids. We were good friends but we lost touch.'

Rob gulped his drink. 'That must have been in the children's home.'

'That's right,' said Kate, wondering what she was getting herself into.

'So you're an orphan too?' he asked. 'That's a shame. A real shame.'

Kate felt awful, telling lies like this. She had to go on now though. 'It wasn't so bad in the home. They treated us OK.'

Rob sighed sadly. 'Julie always wanted to belong to a family. She dreamed of finding her mother one day. She even wrote away for details of her birth. She was thrilled when she got a reply. But all it gave was her mother's name, not where she was living. I can't remember the name now.'

'It doesn't matter,' said Kate, wishing Rob would talk about the more recent past. She wanted to know why he and Julie had split up. These old memories weren't much help.

'Poor kid,' said Rob. 'She was looking forward to trying to find her mother. She never got the chance. She shouldn't have died like that.'

'No,' said Kate. 'I agree with you. Now don't you think it's time you went home, Rob? Come on, we'll share a taxi.'

7

Next day, Kate began to have doubts. There seemed to be no clear way forward. Maybe she was chasing after a shadow. Perhaps Julie had simply died by accident after all.

That night she went again to hear the band. It was fun anyway. Rob came over to say hello. He thanked Kate for listening to his troubles last night. 'Sorry if I was a bore,' he said.

'Don't worry about it,' said Kate with a smile. 'I hope you feel better today.'

'By the way,' said Rob, 'I remembered that name.'

'What name?' asked Kate, puzzled.

'The name I couldn't remember. You know – Julie's mother. The one she was trying to find. It was Mary Ryan. Not that it matters now. Oh well, I'd better get back. See you later!'

Kate sat back to listen to the music but suddenly there was a voice in her ear.

'What was all that about?'

Kate jumped. It wasn't a voice she expected to hear away from the office. David Farley was smiling at her. He looked quite different tonight. In the office he wore a suit. Now he was in a T-shirt and jeans. He looked good in them too.

'I didn't know you were a fan,' he said to Kate.

He sounded pleased. Kate could guess why. The more people who liked the band, the more records they would sell. That was good for business.

David sat at Kate's table. She enjoyed his company. He certainly knew a lot about the music business. And he really believed Easy Money could go to the top. Kate hoped he was right for Alan's sake.

She realised she was beginning to care for Alan. Maybe that wasn't wise. After all, she was here to do a job. Not fall in love with one of the suspects! Some detective I am, thought Kate. I'm not even sure there is a crime to solve.

However, she decided to find out how David Farley felt about Julie's death. How well had he known her?

'Wasn't there another girl who sang with this band?' she asked. 'Didn't she die a short time ago?'

David looked at her. There was shock on his face and deep pain in his brown eyes. Now Kate felt sorry. She hadn't meant to upset him. He must have really cared about Julie.

'Yes,' said David quietly. 'There was another singer. Her name was Julie Rogers. I was going to make her a star. Her death was tragic. Do you mind if we don't talk about it?'

Kate had plenty to think about now. She was sure David meant every word. He looked really upset. She wondered if he had been secretly in love with Julie.

This case was hard to solve. Julie Rogers had meant a lot to many people during her short life. Everyone seemed to like her, even love her.

But somebody hadn't, Kate told herself grimly. Julie had believed that someone was planning to kill her. If it was true, that person tried twice before doing it at last.

The trouble was, Kate felt as far as ever from finding the murderer.

8

Alan phoned Kate the next day.

'Great news,' he told her. 'We're going to make our first record. How would you like to come to the studio? I'd really like you to be there.'

Kate was thrilled. She'd never seen a record being made. She was pleased Alan wanted to share it with her.

'I'd love to come,' she told him. 'Just tell me where.'

The recording studio was on the top floor of a large office block. Kate took the lift. She looked out over London from a window. It was a great view. The River Thames lay far below. It looked like a blue ribbon with toy boats on it.

Kate went down a corridor and found the studio. The band was already there. They were getting ready. Kate saw Alan and gave him a wave. He winked at her and grinned.

Everyone was in a good mood. Rob looked excited and Patsy's eyes shone with happiness. This was their big chance and they all knew it.

David Farley was there to see all went well. Sunset Records hoped to do well with this new group. Kate saw how David kept the band calm and cheerful. He made jokes to Patsy and Alan and gave Rob a friendly pat on the shoulder. He was very good at his job. He took a real interest. It was clear he wasn't only in it for the money.

At last it was time for the big song – 'Voices in the Dark'. This was the one that could be a real hit.

Kate held her breath as the music swelled out. It was a great tune. She listened as Patsy sang:

> What do you hear
> As you lie there alone?
> Only voices in the dark.

At the end, Rob had his guitar solo. It was one of the best bits of the song. Suddenly, he had to stop playing. A string had broken on his guitar. He was very annoyed.

'Don't worry, Rob. We'll take it again from the start,' said David with a smile. He didn't want Rob to get nervous, thought Kate. It would spoil everything.

Rob went across the studio to fetch his spare guitar. He always kept it handy, in case there was a problem.

'OK guys,' said Rob with a grin. 'Let's go.'

These were the last words he ever spoke. As he plugged his guitar into the electric socket, there was a loud crackling noise. Kate and the others watched in horror. A terrible scream turned their blood to ice. There was silence. A strong burning smell hung in the air.

No one spoke. Everyone was stunned.

'What in God's name . . .' said Alan. Patsy began to cry. Kate looked round at all the shocked faces. No one had expected this.

David put his arm round Patsy. He was in charge so it was up to him to decide what to do.

'We'd better phone 999,' he said. 'Police and ambulance. Not that they'll be able to do anything. I'm afraid Rob is dead.'

9

That day was like a nightmare. The police came and asked them lots of questions. They took Rob's body away. They also took the guitar – what was left of it.

No one knew what to do now. Everyone was talking about the terrible accident. Kate felt very alone. Was she the only one who felt like this?

She couldn't believe that this death was an accident too. First Julie, now Rob. What was happening to this band?

But why would anyone kill Rob? How was it done? Above all, who would do a thing like this? There must be something behind it all.

Kate longed to talk to Alan about it. They were such good friends. Maybe they would be more than that one day. Surely she could trust Alan?

Then she thought again. The truth was she couldn't trust anyone. If someone did kill Julie and Rob, it must be someone close to the band. Very close. No, she couldn't risk telling Alan her doubts.

All the next day at work, Kate felt very lonely. She began to be sorry she had got mixed up in all this.

After all, she wasn't a real detective. Maybe she had made a mistake trying to find out about Julie's death.

The office was very quiet that day. News of Rob's death had spread fast. Everyone at Sunset Records was sad about it. Especially David Farley. He looked more upset than anyone.

Kate and Alan met after work. They went to a café and had coffee. They didn't talk much. It was just a comfort to be together. They didn't stay long. Alan seemed very tired. Maybe it was the shock, Kate thought. She felt quite tired herself. She said goodbye to Alan and caught her train home.

Kate took out her front door key. Then she saw something in her bag. She hadn't put it there. She'd never seen it before. It looked like a letter. She went into her flat and took out the white envelope.

Her heart began to race. She wasn't sure why. Something told her this was important. Kate tore open the envelope and took out the slip of paper inside. There were only a few words on it. But they jumped out at her:

'IF YOU WANT TO KNOW HOW ROB DIED, COME TO THE STUDIO AT MIDNIGHT TONIGHT.'

It wasn't signed. Suddenly Kate felt scared. How did the letter get into her bag? She took her bag everywhere with her.

Then she remembered something and it made her feel a little sick. That evening in the café she'd left her bag for a few minutes with Alan. She'd gone to make a phone call. Alan could have put the letter in then. But why would he? Unless he knew a lot more than he had told her.

Kate thought hard. She didn't like the look of this note. It smelt like a trap. But what choice did she have?

I'll have to go tonight, thought Kate. I can't give up now. I wanted to be a detective and maybe now I'm getting close to the truth. I only wish I knew what the truth was.

She dressed with care that night. She took a couple of things that might be useful. Her jacket had deep pockets, which was very handy. Then she caught the late night train to the other side of London. That was where the studio was.

The train made a noise like thunder through the dark tunnels. Kate's heart seemed to hammer just as loudly. She had an uneasy feeling that she was travelling straight into danger.

10

Kate felt jumpy with nerves. She might be walking straight into a trap. Whoever sent that letter knew something about Rob's death. It could even be from the murderer.

I don't know why I'm doing this, Kate said to herself. I must be mad.

She tried to stop worrying and picked up a magazine from the next seat. It was a glossy one with lots of pictures and photos. Not the kind of magazine Kate liked at all. But maybe it would take her mind off her fears. It was called 'Show Business Gossip'. Kate saw a heading – 'Secrets of the Stars'.

She read the page without really taking it in. Her mind was still on the risks she was taking.

Suddenly, something clicked in Kate's brain. It was like finding the last piece of a jigsaw puzzle. Everything fell into place. It didn't make her feel any safer though. Now she was more afraid than ever. She knew how much danger might be waiting for her at the studio.

At last the train stopped at the station. Kate got out and began the walk to the meeting place. In a way she didn't want to get there. She didn't feel very brave but she made herself walk to the studio building. It stretched high above her into the night sky. It wasn't long before midnight and it was very dark. She shivered in the night air.

Kate tried the front door. To her surprise, it wasn't locked. She took the lift up to the top floor. The hum of the lift sounded strange in the empty building. She walked along silent corridors, thinking how spooky it was at night. She could almost feel someone waiting for her.

The door of the studio wasn't locked either. Kate pushed it open. The room was dark but a little moonlight came in through the window. It was just enough to show someone sitting in a chair.

Kate couldn't see who it was. The face was in shadow. But she didn't have to see. Kate had a pretty good idea who was waiting for her.

'Hello, David,' she said. She hoped her voice sounded cool and in control. She certainly didn't feel it.

He bent forward and put on a desk light. David Farley's face looked weird in the dim glow. He looked like a ghost.

'I knew you'd come,' he told Kate. 'You've always wanted to know too much. Always asking questions. This time, you've asked too many.'

Kate's mouth felt dry. 'I've got one more question to ask,' she said.

David smiled but his eyes were cold. 'You're a clever girl. I admit that. But you shouldn't poke your nose into other people's business. What is it you want to know?'

Kate swallowed hard. There was a lump in her throat. It was from fear.

'I think I know why you killed Julie,' she said. 'But I don't know why you killed Rob. What did he ever do to you?'

David laughed. It was a nasty sneering laugh. He was so different from the man Kate knew at work. Of course, this was the real David Farley.

'Rob was a fool,' he said to Kate. 'A stupid fool. He didn't know how much he knew. He didn't know what it meant. But then I heard him talking to you about it. I couldn't take a chance, could I?'

'You mean about Julie's mother, of course,' said Kate.

David sighed. 'It was a pity. I quite liked Rob. But he had to go.'

'How did you do it?' asked Kate. 'How did you manage to kill him?'

David smiled. 'It wasn't hard to fix the guitar so it would give an electric shock. I made sure the other one had a weak string, too. It was child's play, really.' He looked very pleased with himself.

'And Julie?' asked Kate.

David's face changed. Once more, Kate saw a look of pain on his face.

'I was sorry about Julie,' said David. 'I really loved her. She loved me too. We kept it secret from the others. It would have been difficult to work with Rob. Everything was fine until she told me her plans. She wanted to find her mother. That was when I knew I had to kill her.'

Kate remembered the magazine she had read on the train. 'A poor Irish girl called Mary Ryan had a baby. Later, that girl became Maria Ridley, the famous film star. Isn't that right?'

David nodded. 'That's right. I don't know how you know. But I had to stop Julie before she found out. I couldn't risk it. My aunt's a millionaire and I'm her only relative. If a long-lost daughter turned up, I'd have lost everything. You do see that, don't you? I had no choice.'

Kate said nothing. She felt sick and angry at the way Julie Rogers had met her end. And all because of money.

'How did you do it?' she asked.

'It wasn't difficult,' said David Farley. 'We went for a picnic in the country. It was my idea. Julie was very happy that day. Right up to the end. She didn't take long to drown. The water's deep there and she couldn't swim. I knew that, of course.'

Kate's blood ran cold. This man was a monster. And there was every chance she would be his next victim.

11

Kate felt as if she was frozen to the spot. Her feet wouldn't move. Her voice seemed to have gone. She felt like a rabbit in front of a snake. Just waiting for it to strike.

David moved towards her. His eyes gleamed in the lamplight. He looked mad now. Completely mad. Kate knew she was looking at the face of a killer.

She felt herself being pulled over to the window. She couldn't do a thing about it. He was too strong. David opened the window and cold air rushed in. Kate felt it on her face. It woke her from her trance. She looked down. The lights of London twinkled far below. Kate saw how high up they were. It made her dizzy for a moment.

'It's a long way to fall, isn't it?' he said. His voice was like velvet.

'Yes,' Kate's voice was a croak. Fear turned her legs to water. She felt herself being picked up and held in front of the open window. It was clear what David was going to do next.

Kate grabbed her mobile phone from her pocket and tried to dial. David laughed and knocked it out of her hand. Kate looked down and saw the mobile spinning through the air. She felt cold with horror as it smashed to pieces on the ground.

At last, Kate found her voice. 'Don't throw me out, David. Please.' Kate's hand was in her pocket as she spoke.

David smiled a cold smile. 'I'm sorry, Kate. It's a pity you got in the way. You know too much. I can't let you get away now. Don't worry. It'll be a quick death. Just like Julie.'

These words filled Kate with anger. This gave her strength and made her brave. Her hand came quickly out of her pocket. It held a small plastic box. She tore off the lid and threw what was inside into his face. He gave a roar and dropped her on the floor.

Kate was on her feet in a moment. She looked at him. His eyes swam with water and he sneezed again and again. He was blind for a minute. That minute was all Kate needed. She ran to the door and in a moment was running down the corridor.

The pepper had saved her life. But for how long? David would soon be on her track. Kate was afraid to take the lift. He would easily know which floor she was on by the lights. The stairs were slower but they were safer. Besides, she had another trick up her sleeve.

Her heart was thumping in her chest. It sounded like a drum. Then Kate heard another noise behind her. It made her sick with fear. Footsteps behind her. David's footsteps!

Kate got to the stairs at last. She gasped for breath and started down. It was a long way to the ground. She just kept on running. How many more steps were there?

Then she heard the sound she hoped for. The crash of a body falling down the stairs behind her. It had to be David. The cooking oil she had put on the steps hadn't let her down.

Slowly, quietly, Kate crept back upstairs. He lay on the landing between two floors. His leg was at an odd angle beneath him. Probably broken, Kate thought. She looked down at him and his eyes opened. They were filled with such hate that Kate shivered.

'I'll get you for this!' he said, spitting the words out at her.

Kate was very calm now. 'I don't think so, David. You won't be able to move for some time. Not with that leg. You don't mind if I borrow your mobile phone?'

She bent down and picked it up. It had fallen out of his pocket. 'Thanks. I just want to phone the police. We've got quite a lot to tell them, haven't we?'